The Almost Mothers

Laura Besley

First published 2020 by Dahlia Publishing Ltd
6 Samphire Close Hamilton
Leicester LE5 1RW
ISBN 9781913624002

Some of the stories in this collection have appeared elsewhere, in a slightly different form:

'All the Children' in *Lunate*, 'Breaking the Seal' in *Spelk*,
'Near and Far' in *Spelk*, 'That Apple' in *Fictive Dream*,
'The Motherhood Contract' in *Ellipsis*

Printed and bound by Grosvenor Group

A CIP catalogue record for this book is
available from The British Library

Contents

To all mothers, especially the almost ones.

Mothers Anonymous

We're not here to judge, they tell us. Night after night we sit in this cold church hall sipping teas and coffees, trying to get the good biscuits before they're all gone. We're here to support each other, they tell us. We're here to listen.

Sheila, the woman who runs it, wears so many bangles she's like a walking percussionist and I have to fight the urge to strangle her. She radiates warmth and love and acceptance and I think: why did you get my share? Did you steal it from me in a former life? I'd rather talk to someone cynical and bitter. Someone who might understand.

I'm ten days off my first annual coin. Haven't missed a meeting yet. Tonight there's a new woman. She's going to talk. I've learned to spot them: women who come in with the words bubbling up inside them, ready to burst.

Sure enough she volunteers to talk, stands even though she doesn't have to, and we all chant 'Welcome to our safe circle!' like fucking hippies. I look at the floor; I don't want to see her face as she utters the usual.

'I'm Melissa,' she says in a raspy voice like she smokes a pack a day. It makes me look up and before I know it she is staring right back at me. 'And I hate being a mother.'

Playing at Being Grown-Ups

'Fuck me. You look like shit!' Stacey slides into the seat next to me.

'Some friend you are.'

'Just telling you how it is. How did it go?'

'Alright.'

She blows a bubble with her baby pink gum.

If I wasn't so tired, I'd reach out and pop it. Instead, I watch it expand until pale stretchmarks appear. It bursts, a saggy mass on Stacey's lip until she sucks it back in.

'Jenny said they did loads together,' Stacey says.

'Whatever.' I yawn openly.

'She took her to the playground and the petting zoo.'

She scrapes her chair closer to mine, 'How was it really?'

'Awful.' I rub my eyes. 'It didn't stop crying all bloody weekend. I tried everything. I bounced, rocked, sang. I was up all night. It didn't nap during the day so by midnight I put it in the garage.'

'You did what?'

'It's fine. I could hear the cries faintly through the floorboards but not enough to wake me up.'

Stacey stares at me. 'It's going to show that you left her. Psychologists say–'

'I don't care.' I shake my head. 'I used the cry it out method. Loads of people do it.'

'Not in the garage!'

'Who's going to know it was in there?'

'Proximity to Primary Carer.'

'I was in the room above. Technically that's less than five metres away.'

'Temperature.'

'Shit! I didn't think of that.'

'If you fail the Weekend Care one more time, you'll have to do the advanced course. And if you fail that…'

'I know. I'll be labelled unfit to be a mother.' I do the thing with my fingers in the air, mainly to cover my face and tears.

'Shh!' She glances around her. 'Don't say that. Don't ever let anyone hear you say that.'

'Morning, everyone.' Mrs Knight claps her hands as she walks into the classroom, her reading glasses bobbing on her too tight blouse, and stops behind the desk where the baby is lying. I know what it's wearing under the snowsuit because I dressed it this morning. Now it's quiet, and I can hand it back, I can summon a little affection. There were some giggles on Saturday afternoon when we were playing peekaboo. I wonder if that will go in my favour?

When Mrs Knight switches on the interactive whiteboard behind her, a collection of pie charts and graphs appear and the class collectively gasps.

'Hmm. Let's have a look at how you got on, shall we?'

Getting Ahead

8.42 is the perfect time to arrive at school. Exactly three minutes before the gates open. Any earlier and the children get bored and start being silly. Any later and you're just asking to be late. No one wants to be last.

I'm pushing the buggy, Oliver trotting along next to it, thinking I've timed my arrival this morning to perfection, when up ahead, I see Susan. 'Come on,' I say, upping the pace.

'Mummy, you're going too fast,' Oliver says. The whine in his voice, immediately grating.

'No, I'm not. Look, there's Joe. Don't you want to catch up with him?'

'Mummeeee, I can't,' he says and sits down on the pavement. I see Susan's red coat disappear round a corner. I yank Oliver to his feet and crouch down to his height. 'You will move faster,' I say in my don't-mess-with-me whisper. The whisper works wonders and no-one can accuse you of shouting.

Oliver gets up and starts walking, but the momentum is lost and the chance of catching up with Susan is nil. Unless. Do I spot little Ruth jumping up and down in a puddle? (Peppa Pig's got a lot to answer for.) Oh yes, I do. I sidle up.

'Oh dear,' I say, noticing little Ruth's tights are covered in mud. 'What's going on here?'

Ruth jumps one more time and a big gush of water plops into one of her wellies. She starts crying. That's what happens when you don't put them in a buggy, I think. Susan's always so high and mighty about her three-year-old walking the bigger one to school.

'Can I help?'

'No, it's fine,' Susan says, reaching a hand out to Ruth. 'I have spares. Obviously.'

'Obviously.'

This is why you need a three-minute leeway.

We round the final corner, the multi-coloured school gates are only a few feet away. She's walking next to me, but then speeds up a little, but my buggy wheels are still in front of her. We go through the gates side by side.

'Oliver has gone up to reading level pink.' I unhook his book bag from one of the buggy handles.

Susan smooths Joe's hair with her mittened hands. (I know she has to wear mittens to get Joe to wear his mittens. I have gloves on.) 'Really?'

'Yes. Is Joe still on blue?'

'Yes, but he's going to Spanish classes once a week and they say speaking a second language can delay a child initially, but in the long-run it's very good for them.'

'Spanish? We've been looking into Oliver learning Mandarin.' I reach under the buggy for his flask. 'It'll open up so many opportunities for him in Asia in the future.'

'I don't think I'd want my children travelling so far away. That's why we chose Spanish.'

'South America's probably as far away as Asia. Maybe even further.' I put Oliver's book bag and flask on the relevant shelves outside the classroom.

'Joe can add up now,' Susan says, unzipping his coat.

'I'm sure Oliver can too.' I'm sure he can't. 'I just haven't asked him recently.' I have. He definitely can't do it. Oliver unzips his own coat. 'Well done, Oliver, for unzipping your own coat,' I say, a smile spreading quickly across my face. Then he shrugs it off and throws it on the floor. My smile evaporates.

'Oliver, darling,' Susan says, 'hang your coat up on your peg like Joe's done.' And sure enough I look over and Joe is hanging up his own coat. On the right peg.

I guide Oliver over to his peg and quickly stuff his hat and scarf into the sleeves while Susan's got her back turned. Done.

The teacher appears. 'Good morning, everyone. In you come.' There is a flurry of goodbyes, hugs and kisses, but Oliver is nowhere to be seen. He's gone in without saying goodbye. Tears well and I berate myself for being so silly. Apparently, it's a good sign. it means he's confident or so I read in a parenting magazine. I look over at Susan and her face is a mirror image of mine.

'He didn't say goodbye,' she says.

I walk over to her and put my arm around her shoulders. 'Do you want to come to mine for a coffee?'

She nods and we walk out of the school gates together. Neck and neck.

Near and Far

And there she lies. On stark white sheets, stripped of her accessories – make-up, jewellery, entitlement – she no longer looks like the woman I knew.

'Your mother might not make it through the night,' the doctor says.

'Right,' I say, turning to face him. No white coat, the buttons on his cardigan are not with their rightful partners. He scribbles something on a chart and leaves.

Sitting on the edge of a plastic chair, I reach out to take her hand, then pull back. I can hear cicadas calling, smell jasmine flowers. I'm dancing barefoot in the garden, heat enveloping me. Cook is singing in the kitchen, tutting indulgently as I steal another lemper ayam, the wonderful combination of sweet sticky rice and spicy shredded chicken exploding in my mouth. Suddenly I'm forced into shoes too tight, clothes too itchy, in a country that's too cold. Home, apparently.

Machines emit an unrushed beat.

My mother. That title given to her due to a technicality because she pushed me out into this world. In my first days I barely slept, barely ate, but after a week we were discharged. Cook could hear me crying from the end of the driveway and wrapped me in a scarf, nestled me into the folds of her body. I was asleep within minutes. Maybe my mother took it as a personal slight, but from that moment on she kept her distance.

And yet here I am, by her bedside as she takes her last breaths. A daughter's duty.

In the early hours of the morning, the steady rhythm transforms into a continuous sound. 'I'm sorry,' the doctor says. 'Your mother has passed away.'

I nod, but think no. My mother passed away years ago, alone, and nobody thought to tell me.

Everything's Fine

Don't fall asleep. Don't fall asleep, don't fall asleep.

'You can get up now, Mrs Edwards,' the doctor says, the sound of rubber gloves being snapped off. 'That scar is healing nicely.'

I force myself to open my eyes, to sit up, stand up, get dressed.

'That final course of antibiotics has obviously done the trick.' He is typing, head tilted back to see through his crescent-moon glasses, and doesn't look at me.

'Good,' I say, pulling on my coat. I see a face and step back, knocking over a bin, when I realise it's me. The new me. The she who doesn't wear make-up, have time to wash or sometimes even brush her hair, the she who often has sick or even poo on her clothes for hours before noticing. The she whose eyes are constantly red from lack of sleep and or crying.

'Is there anything else I can help you with, Mrs Edwards?'

My mouth opens, and closes. Once, twice. *Can you tell me how to do this? Why I thought I'd be able to do this? Can I go back?*

'Mrs Edwards?' He takes off his reading glasses and looks at me.

'I'm fine,' I hear myself say as I leave, closing the door behind me.

Down to Earth

In order to increase our population, I was sent to Earth to obtain information regarding how they have managed to increase their population to 7.7 billion in the same time that we have only increased ours to 385,622. Here are my findings:

- Earth Mothers are only pregnant for nine months;
- Earth Mothers can be pregnant multiple times;
- Earth Mothers can give birth to multiple children at one time;
- If the Earth Mother cannot give birth through the normal channels, another Earth Person (Doctor) can cut her open and put her back together again. Both Earth Mother and Baby Earthling can survive this;
- If the Earth Mother cannot feed her Baby Earthling milk from her body, there is an alternative milk (Formula) which is sufficient at keeping the Baby Earthling alive until it is time for solid food;
- If Baby Earthlings are a little sick, there is a magic liquid that makes them better. This is known as Calpol;
- To stop Baby Earthlings getting really sick, a trained Earth Person (Nurse) sticks a long, metal object (Needle) into them on a semi-regular basis. This contains something known as a vaccination.

Although recommended, this is not compulsory and not all Earth People follow this process;

- There are some illnesses that cannot be cured by Nurses or Doctors;
- Earthlings are not considered adults until they are eighteen years old, although some work before this milestone is reached;
- When Earthlings become old, they are often again totally reliant on others;
- Earthlings kill each other for no reason.

The findings are inconclusive.

All the Children

It's an old wives' tale that pregnancies are harder with boys than with girls, Sylvie thinks as she quietly opens the lid of the old tea chest. She's been pregnant five times: four with boys and once with a girl. In the summer months before her eldest son was born, Sylvie spent the evenings sewing outfits and when she got too big to bend over the sewing machine, she started knitting. Arthur used to joke that they could clothe the whole street with the number of outfits she made. Not knowing the sex of their child, she made the smallest outfits in white, green and yellow, and bigger ones in blues and pinks. She could never have known that the pink ones would spend the next ten years buried away.

Carefully she lifts out the baby clothes wrapped in pink tissue paper. Her youngest, three months old today, is lying in the middle of the double bed, kicking and gurgling. The room smells of baby shampoo and talc and that sweet milky smell that only babies have. Soon it will be naptime and Sylvie will nap too, a luxury since the eldest three are at school. When Christopher was a baby, she didn't take the opportunity to sleep during the day, there always seemed too much to do, and after that she always had another one to look after when the baby was napping.

'Let's see what these look like on you, shall we?' she says, stroking the baby's cheek. She manoeuvres pudgy arms into a little pink cardigan. 'You look beautiful. Yes, you do.' She lies down on the bed and shuts her eyes.

She wakes to the sound of Arthur pounding up the stairs. Her first thought is joy, the joy she always feels when she thinks about being in this house instead of living above the shop. But panic soon washes away the joy and she shuffles to the end of the bed, shielding the baby from view.

'Hello, love,' Arthur whispers, pushing the door open. 'I hope I didn't wake you.'

'It's alright. I've got things to do.' She reaches up to pat down her wavy blonde hair, her hand trembling like a willow in a gale. 'I wasn't expecting you.'

'The shop was quiet. I left Fred in charge.' Arthur looks at the sleeping baby, whose snores are barely audible. 'Oh Sylvie.' He lowers himself onto the bed and pulls her towards him.

Sylvie collapses against him, tears collecting in the crevices around her eyes.

'Julie's gone, love,' he says. 'Don't think I don't miss her too, because I do, but we have to move on.'

The snoring stops and Sylvie lays a hand on the blanket to check that the little chest is still rising and falling.

Arthur hands her a neatly folded handkerchief and she presses it to her cheeks, inhaling washing detergent, and unwavering love.

'This baby will never replace her,' Arthur says, 'and I know you were hoping for another girl, but look at him... He's lovely.'

'Yes,' she says, threading the handkerchief between her fingers, 'yes, I suppose he is.'

Wish Upon a Star

Be careful what you wish for, my grandmother used to say.

I wished for chocolate cake and ballet lessons and for Neil O'Brien to hold my hand.

Morning light waves at me from behind the curtains when I wake. Isabelle has finally slept through. It will take more than one night to feel rested, but I feel human at last.

I hum to myself as I pull on my dressing gown, shoving my feet into slippers. Humming some tune I'd heard on the radio that I didn't particularly like.

She looks so beautiful. A source of anxiety and joy and love. I stroke her cheek. It feels cold, but it is winter. She doesn't stir. There is no movement of the head. No twitch of her hand. No flutter of her lashes. She must be in a very deep sleep, I think, and tiptoe back out of the room.

Hooked

'Excuse me,' the security guard said. 'Can I check your receipt?

'Of course,' she said.

She never planned to do it again, let alone make a habit of it, but she became addicted to the rush of feelings. It was a welcome change to the numbness that she'd been experiencing lately. Like all addictions, the initial exhilarations wore off too soon, so she set herself challenges: steal something big, something round, something orange, until she was caught.

It all started rather innocently when she forgot to pay for the milk. Pushing the buggy with one hand and holding the basket with the other, she'd got the items on her list, (bread, bananas, yoghurts, chocolate) as quickly as possible, placating a shouty Henry with biscuits. The basket was full, and heavy, so she'd put the four-pint of milk underneath.

About to fold up the buggy, she discovered her error and could've gone back to rectify it. Instead, using the excuse that she'd already loaded Henry into his car seat and didn't have the energy to get him back out again, she drove home. For the rest of the day she felt delicious, like she used to after having sex in the middle of the day.

'You haven't paid for this.' The guard held up a pair of oven gloves (today's challenge: steal something with an animal on it).

'I'm so sorry,' she said, cheeks reddening as that delicious feeling once again coursed around her body. 'I must've forgotten.'

He escorted her to the Customer Service Desk where she paid for it. Another item she didn't need.

'I won't press charges this time,' he said.

'Thank you,' she said, grateful for the protective cloak of her middle-classness.

'But I won't let it go again.'

She nodded her understanding.

There were always other supermarkets.

Breakthrough in Motherhood Programme

Scientists working at the Leicester Institute for Modern Civilisation believe they have found a cure for unwanted motherhood.

The Unwanted Motherhood programme, estimated to have cost in the region of £1bn, is being welcomed by both the government and private investors.

The new one-off treatment, launched in London today by Prime Minister Tabitha Murray and NHS Chief Executive Surita Singh, can wipe all memories of a baby's existence. It is being offered in conjunction with plastic surgery to remove scarring and stretch marks. TabulaRasa, Latin for 'clean slate', is set to save the NHS millions in time-consuming talking therapies.

Surita Singh said: "It is a simple and cost effective procedure."

Keira Taylor, 27, a mother from West Barley, says she can't wait to have try the therapy: "I haven't had a good night's sleep since the baby was born. I either have nightmares or the baby wakes up. I badly need a good night's sleep. This breakthrough will mean I'm free at last."

A commitment to the unwanted children is at the heart of the plan. They will be placed with one of the many couples who are not able to conceive naturally.

Recent figures released by The Office for National Statistics reveal that there are over half a million unwanted pregnancies a year.

Health Minister Roger Perryman, said: "This will reduce the number of backstreet abortions, which pose an obvious risk to women's health. It's a no-brainer."

However, some experts have voiced concerns about the treatment. Dr Michael Chang, Head of Psychology at Durham University has described it as "inhumane".

He said that the measures outlined go against what make us human.

Tiffany Burgess CEO, of the charity Misguided or Unwanted Motherhood Support said. "This undermines everything MUMS is trying to achieve. We work with mothers, by giving them someone to talk to and providing practical support, to enable them to be better parents. More often than not the results are very positive."

She raised the question of what will happen when these children look for their birth mothers and discover that they have no memory of them. "It could be devastating for both the mother and the child."

The government will keep confidential records of all wiped memories.

How to Grow Your Own Baby

You will need:

a clear trough (50cms x 30cms x 40cms)

Instructions:

1. Plant the seed in dark soil, 10cm deep.
2. Place in a sunny spot, but not direct sunlight.
3. Water with exactly ten millilitres per day.
4. Talk and sing to stimulate growth.
5. After nine months, your baby will be ready.

Share your progress with us. Post a photo on Instagram with the hashtag #BarrenBeBanished

That Face

A face moves into my line of vision and its mouth, painted in red lipstick, opens. 'Lynda, hi!' The face has deep crow's feet, only enhanced by heavy make-up. 'It is Lynda, isn't it?'

My head nods, as if of its own accord.

Her index finger points at the chest below the face. 'I'm Amanda.' The hand, with a rather large diamond catching the harsh supermarket light, reaches out to squeeze my arm. 'From school.'

I look at the hand still resting on my arm and know that social etiquette dictates that this is fine, just fine, but I have to resist not to shake it off.

'You haven't changed a bit.'

This is a lie. Yesterday I happened to be looking at photos from five years ago in Thailand, when I was still with Ian. Who is she kidding?

'Obviously I have,' her mouth says, and her hand moves from my arm to smooth her short bob.

'Hmm,' I say, unsure whether she wants me to agree with her or not.

'So, how are you?' She tilts her head a little to the left.

'Fine. Fine. You?'

'Good. I live in Windsor now with hubby and the babies.' Her eyes do that thing where they go soft and dewy. 'I say babies,' she smiles, 'they're eight, six and four. Hardly babies. But they'll always be babies to me, you know?'

I'm trying to think of something to say. Something to stop her mouth motoring towards the inevitable. 'What are you doing here, then?' is what I come up with. No enquiry about names, sex, the child CVs of hobbies and achievements.

'I'm visiting my mother. She still lives in the area.'

'That's nice. Sorry, Amanda, I'm in a bit of a hurry.' The glossy highlights in my blow-dried hair telling another story.

'Got to get home?'

'Uh huh,' I say.

'To the kids?'

Bam! She's done it. Well done her.

'I don't have–.'

Her mouth forms a perfect Oh, but no sound comes out. I leave before her face turns into *that face*. Can't stand that face.

2056: A New Generation

I look at my daughter and I know.

I notice her fuller face, fuller breasts.

I watch the small mouthfuls of food she's chewing, chewing, chewing, before struggling to swallow.

I notice that she washes each mouthful down with a sip of mint water.

I look at her and I know.

After lunch I take her hand and ask how she's feeling.

'A bit queasy, but also really hungry and really tired. Do you think I'm sick?'

It's been years since I've seen anyone in this state, but my medical training leaves me in no doubt. 'No, darling.' I take a deep breath. 'I think you might be pregnant.'

'Preg…nant?'

She stumbles over the word. I wonder when the last time was that she heard it, let alone said it.

'You mean I've got a baby growing inside me?'

'Yes.'

'That's impossible, Mama.'

Her voice is steady, but the fact that my forty-year old daughter has used her childhood name for me betrays her fear.

'Not impossible. Who have you had intercourse with recently?'

'Just the usuals.' A lack of procreation has largely meant the end of monogamy.

'No-one new?'

She shakes her head.

I hear the faint ring of the bell from the building across the road.

I used to hear that same bell ring and know what it meant; start of school; lunchtime; end of playtime; end of the day.

I remember the announcement that the school was closing. In the four years between my daughter and my son attending, numbers in the classes had halved, rapidly dwindling to none.

I remember listening to the news that all schools were going to be renovated into Assisted Living accommodation, a cross between a retirement home and a hospital. Keeping all the elderly alive is very expensive. Soon there won't be anyone working. Soon there won't be anyone at all. Unless…

I can still hear my father's words when I was applying to medical school. 'Preeti, you should become a gynaecologist. Women will always be having babies.' He'd turn in his grave if he knew.

I take my daughter up to the attic where my old equipment is stashed. I lift a machine out of its box and plug it in. 'Sit down over there,' I say to her and rub the wand over her stomach. The room is filled with the rhythm of a very fast train.

'What's that?' she asks.

'Your baby's heartbeat,' I whisper, feeling like my own is trying to catch up.

'What do I do, Mama?'

I look at my daughter and I can't possibly know how this will end, but I can hope. 'We wait and see, sweetheart.'

The Almost Mother

'Is it true?'

She turned at the sound of Callum's voice. He was staring at her, eyes dark and face pale. She opened her mouth to say, 'Is what true?' but she couldn't make the words come out. She knew, without asking, what he meant and she was unprepared.

She'd almost forgotten how it had happened. She'd met Steve on a Tuesday at work. Not her normal day, but someone had been sick. Steve was a year older than her, but looked younger. Certainly too young to have a baby. But he did have a baby, a boy called Callum. She'd never expected Callum to call her Mummy. Never modelled it, but somehow it just happened. And after what had happened to his birth mother, everyone was fine with it. For months, her Claire's heart hammered whenever he called her that, but over time it quietened and became normal. She almost forgot herself. Almost.

'Callum,' she said, wiping her hands on her apron. He started crying. She hadn't seen him cry for so long. She couldn't remember the last time. Just like you don't know when the last time they'll kiss you on the lips will be, or crawl onto your lap for a cuddle. But that kind of letting go is gradual, normal.

She'd forgotten how hard it is when you have to shatter their worlds. Sorry, darling, the Easter bunny is make believe. The tooth fairy doesn't really live in Aunt Tracey's shed. And Father Christmas doesn't actually exist. He'd been hurt, ferocious in his reactions, shouting: You lied to me, Mum. You lied. You said you'd always tell me the truth. Steve soothed her again, saying: everyone learns these truths and survives. It's just part of growing up. But she always knew there was a bigger truth lurking behind all those other untruths.

She took a step towards Callum, this almost-man who'd never looked more like a little boy, arms outstretched. Despite having been taller than her for over a year, she hoped he would slot into her body like he always had and she could hug his pain away. Instead, he walked past her and slammed the door behind him.

Supermum

Finally it's my turn. I walk into the tent. It's dark with vanilla-scented candles in large glass jars dotted around, and there she is: slim, beautifully made-up, nails perfectly manicured, hair hanging in luscious locks down her back. It's Super Mum.

'Hello,' she says, voice as soft as a baby's cheek.

Is that a whiff of coffee I detect? I'm cold after standing out in the autumn drizzle for hours and my coffee radar is on high alert. No, it can't be. Super Mum doesn't drink caffeine. She doesn't need it.

'Hello.' My palms are clammy, my voice cracks.

'How can I help you be the perfect mummy?'

'I have two children: Zara who's six and Daniel who's four.' I'm naturally short-tempered, but was led to believe that once I became a mummy all my faults would disappear, like Super Mum's did. 'And I'd like to be calmer.'

'Yes, I can understand. Being calm is very important in raising stable and secure children.' She reaches behind her for one of her five parenting books and puts it on the table between us. Her big smile, as well as the three mini-smiles of her perfect children: Jasper, Poppy and Quentin, look up at me from the glossy cover. 'There's a whole section on being calm in here,' she says.

I nod. 'I've read your book. I've read all of your books.'

'Thank you. I'm so pleased. Did you like them?'

'Oh, yes. It's just… I was wondering, if you had any further advice on how to be calm. I've tried the three steps and the breathing exercises and making up funny words. But nothing seems to work for me.'

'That's a concern.' She furrows her brows.

'I sometimes…' I swallow, ignoring the knot in my stomach and decide to bare my soul, since this may be a once in a lifetime opportunity (especially considering the cost of the tickets) to get advice from the mighty Super Mum. 'I sometimes,' I lean in as I say this, 'shout.'

A look of pity spreads across her face, its implications like sticky peanut butter-covered fingers. 'That is a shame. You do know that shouting can permanently damage your children, don't you?'

'I know,' I say, feeling like I'm back at school and being told off by my favourite teacher. 'That's why I want to stop it. How do I stop it?'

She picks up her book. 'Read it,' she says. After flipping a few pages, she runs a purple nail down the index. 'Chapters 10 to 13. Everything you need to know is in there.'

'I've read the book.' I don't even bother disguising a sigh.

'You'll know what to do then.' She glances at her watch. 'I'm afraid our time is up.' And as if by magic another equally glossy person materialises and opens the back flap of the tent. 'It was nice to meet you.'

'And you,' I say, blinking at the sudden light and the tears in my eyes.

I follow the signs to the toilets, slide a lock across the furthest stall and sit on the closed lid. My feet pulled up, I rest my head on my knees and let the tears fall. If Super Mum can't help me, who can?

A few minutes later, I hear the door open and close, a tap run. The chirp of a mobile phone clatters around the room.

'Jasper, darling, how are you?' I hear, the voice familiar from only a few moments ago.

Silence.

'You've done what? You bloody idiot! What on earth did you do that for? Stay there. I'll be home soon.'

To Cut a Long Story Short

She asks you how you are and you notice how nicely her hair is made-up and her make-up is in all the right places and you try to remember how to answer that question, partly because it's been so long since you've had a conversation with an adult but also because you're having one of those days, you know, the ones where the baby won't nap, it starts to rain as soon as you finish hanging the washing out, the baby still won't nap, you burn lunch, spill your tea, run out of chocolate so you go to the corner shop and despite it having been dry since you got the washing in, as soon as you go outside it starts to rain again, but you figure it'll be ok because the walk will send the baby off to sleep and then you can have your chocolate with a cup of tea on the sofa and the baby can nap in the pram in the kitchen, but then you remember that the kettle is in the kitchen and after you've oh-so-carefully maneuvered the pram inside, you're not going to risk waking the baby by boiling the kettle, so you unplug it and boil it on the landing, rush downstairs for milk, hold your breath as the fridge hums and omits light, but it's okay, the baby stays asleep and you creep back upstairs and decide, actually, to take your tea and chocolate to bed, you get in and you've been horizontal for, maybe, 4.3 seconds when you hear the baby cry and you want to cry too, you want to scream and cry, and cry some more, but you don't because if you start, you'll never stop, so you check your watch and think: she's already in the pram, I'll go to playgroup, so you get out of bed, get your shoes and coat on and go, before you can change your mind, and you're slightly delirious when you get there because of all the almost-crying, the lack of sleep and the sugar-rush of two chocolate bars and initially no one talks to you and you nearly cry again, but finally someone asks you how you are and you do that open-mouth, closed-mouth thing a couple of times trying to weigh up how honest to be and then you say, fine, I'm fine.

Breaking the Seal

Daylight creeps into the room, snaking its tendrils of light around the furniture and the sleeping form of my husband. I've been awake since 3:53 and to distract myself I've made a "to do" list: lunchboxes (no meat for Jack!), school run, supermarket shop, Scott's suits from the dry cleaners, pick up the kids, football practice, dinner, bath, bed, tidy the kitchen at some point. Surely that'll keep me busy enough so I don't have to think about what's in the envelope.

I switch off the alarm before its shrillness breaks the silence. Scott always sighs when I set it earlier than necessary, but I like having that extra half hour to myself, before they all get up and start making demands. The plush carpet swallows my footsteps as I pick my way out of the bedroom and down the stairs.

The fat envelope sits on the kitchen counter.

The first day it merely whispered my name. Then it tried shouting. When that failed, it began taunting me, goading me, preying on the marbles of fear clicking and clacking around in my stomach.

I walk past the envelope, make a cup of tea and open the back door. The early morning chill snatches at my warmth and I clasp my cup a little tighter. The problem – as I tried to explain to Scott last night – is that once the information is known, it can't be unknown. Once I've read her name, I won't have any control over it. It'll be there, dancing around my brain like a wind-up ballerina in a jewellery box.

A sparrow lands on the dewy grass and starts pecking at the ground. Am I foolish in thinking that this stranger will fill the gap that's been drilled into my soul by the loss of my parents, the ones who raised me? Or will we have some magical connection, something that has forever been in the shadows of my life and just needs to step out into the light?

I throw the dregs of my tea onto the clematis next to me and watch the sparrow fly up to its family. Not all the fledglings will survive, but year after year this pair come back, instinct telling them that our tree is where their young will get the best chance at a good life.

The envelope is quiet as I sidle up to it, knowing it has won.

That Apple

As you stand in the bathroom with a white plastic stick showing two blue lines, you hear your mother's words over and over again, running through your brain like a mouse trapped in a wheel. Everyone knows that the one thing the daughter of a single mother can't do is fall pregnant at a tender age out of wedlock. It is drummed in from very early on. 'Yes, yes,' you always reply and roll your eyes at your sister, who has also been hearing the same lecture for as long as she can remember.

In a minute, you will have to walk down the stairs, sit at the kitchen table, and try to act as calmly as possible when you tell your mum that unfortunately the apple hasn't fallen far from the tree. You expect your mum to shout and scream. You expect tears, and maybe even smashed crockery. What you don't expect is silence, broken only by the gentle ticking of the clock above the cooker. 'What have I always told you?' said in a deadly whisper is infinitely worse. It hangs above the kitchen table like a black cloud about to burst open and spray you with bone-chilling sleet. You always knew that you were in the deepest trouble when there was whispering.

'And the father?' This is the question you have been dreading most. It would not be anywhere near as bad if the father, if you can already call him that, was a strong, stable and good person, someone who had been in your life for a long time, someone who people looked at with a soft expression on their faces and said, 'he's a good 'un, isn't he?' Or maybe it was someone you had just met, but people looked at the two of you together and said, 'well, that's real love if ever I saw it.' But no. The father of your unborn child is someone you met at a nightclub and you have obviously never talked about having children. But you know, without even asking, that he's not going to be one of those men who "steps up to the plate".

Your mother rubs her face with her ringless hands. 'And are you planning on keeping it?' She looks at you and you can't hold her stare. This question is worse than the father question.

'Uhm, yes,' you reply.

'Uhm, yes?' she parrots. Now the screaming starts. 'Young lady, there is no uhming and ahing in this situation. Having a baby is hard work. The sleepless nights, the crying, the changing, the feeding, giving up any wishes you had for yourself or your future until they're at school. Or worse. You might never get those chances back again. And let's not get started on what being pregnant does to your body. Am I making myself clear?'

'Perfectly.' You look down at your trembling hands and feel a few tears roll down your cheeks and splash onto the red and white checked tablecloth.

'It's not that I didn't love you,' your mother says, 'but being a mother is a huge sacrifice and I just want you to understand that. Having a baby is something you need to be one hundred and ten per cent sure about.'

You nod. Technically, you can't be one hundred and ten per cent sure about anything, but this is not something you feel should be pointing out at this moment.

The back door swings open and your older (not yet knocked up) sister barges into the kitchen and stops abruptly, taking in the drama that is circling the room. 'Uh oh,' she says, still with a smile dancing between her lips and eyes. She won't be smiling soon, you think.

Your mother looks at you and says, 'Well, Beth, this is your news to tell.'

You look at your sister, who has bitten into an apple without washing it first. 'I'm pregnant,' you say, and watch her chew very slowly, eyes still soft but changing from smiling to concerned. And then to your horror you see the flicker of anger whirl around her face before she speaks. 'Oh Beth,' she says, 'how could you?'

'The usual way,' you reply, because you're sure sarcasm is your only saviour right now.

She rolls her eyes. 'Trust you.' And you don't know whether she means the pregnancy or the sarcastic remark.

In Hiding

The doorbell rings and I freeze, one hand clutching a scourer, the other a teacup. Teddy rolls his eyes at me and slinks off to the cupboard under the stairs. I glance in as I pass by: he has some snacks, a flask of water, a torch and his favourite book. He'll be fine for an hour or so. I push the door shut with my foot.

Looking through the spyhole, I see a woman with short brown curls and fuchsia lipstick. I take a deep breath and open the door a fraction.

'Hello,' she says. 'I live next door. Thought I'd come and introduce myself. I'm Trisha.'

'Sarah,' I reach out my hand.

She clasps it and pumps it up and down. 'Can I come in?'

'Of course,' I say, and stand aside to let her into the hallway. I've found it doesn't pay to put these busybodies off. 'Tea?' And by that I mean peppermint leaves in hot water. Gone are the days of black tea.

'Yes please,' she says, walking through to the kitchen. 'Oh, haven't they done this place nice? Mine needs re-doing. I'm on the list.'

Once I've filled the kettle, I root around in my bag for my identity card. I slot it into the card reader and the kitchen light flickers on. I want to turn it off, preserve my meagre rations, but sitting here in the semi-darkness will only arouse suspicion. The kettle starts humming its merry tune.

'I just leave mine in,' she says. 'It's not worth the hassle of constantly taking it in and out.'

'True,' I say, although the less time you're plugged in, the less time they're monitoring you.

'Where've you moved from?'

I put two cups on the table between us and sit down opposite her. 'Up north.'

'You don't sound northern.'

'I'm not from the north originally. I like changing things up.'

'Not me,' she says. 'I'm born and bred here. Know everyone and everything.' She blows on her hot water and takes a sip.

I bet you do, I think.

I knew from the first moment I held him that I wouldn't give him up. Everyone told me I'd have to, when the time came, he would leave the family home to work the land, or the mines, and I'd never see him again. People said I should feel proud that my son would help rebuild this country to its former glory, make it strong again and show the world that we didn't need its support. But I couldn't do it. I'll never see my family again, or my husband, but it'll be worth it to keep Teddy with me.

bell sounds outside, causing the birds to take flight from the leafless tree in the garden.

'Got work at the factory, have you?'

'Yes.' I've been doing factory work for a long time. I wouldn't mind it if I didn't get so bored. Too much time to think, to worry, but it's my only choice.

'A lot of folk work up there. I can introduce you around if you like.'

'That's kind of you.' Couldn't really say anything else.

'I don't work,' she says, sitting a little taller in her seat. 'I have three girls at home to raise. I'm teaching them to cook, clean, wash and iron. My eldest can also knit and sew. They'll make fine wives and mothers one day.'

'I'm sure they will.' I don't ask if she has any boys at home. If she still has any boys at home.

Her cup is halfway to her mouth and she stops. 'That's a terrible smell you've got in here.'

'I'm sure it's nothing.'

'That's not nothing. It smells like s-h-i-t.' She whispers the last word, although I don't know why. One of those women who never swears, not even when there's no-one to hear.

'I'll sort it.'

'Let me help you.' She gets up and starts sniffing around and I'm worried that she's like one of those witches in the Roald Dahl book and will sniff out my child hiding under the stairs.

'Don't worry, Trisha. I don't want to trouble you.' My heart is beating so fast, it feels like it might snap.

'No trouble,' she says. 'I've had four children. I know the smell of s-h-i-t,' another whisper, 'anywhere.' She laughs at her own joke. 'And if we actually find some, we can sell it to the Smyths. They've got that big farm at the end of the lane.' She claps her hand across her mouth, horrified that it's revealed her secrets.

I know people who've been desperate enough to sell their own faeces. Or traded it for some food. British produce, grown in people's shit! You don't see that on the government posters. To be fair, the farmers nearly always buy it. They're desperate too.

I smile, try to reassure her that what she's said doesn't matter, but luckily for me she's embarrassed and wants to leave. 'Oh my gosh,' she says, thundering down the hall, 'look at the time. I'd best get home to get the dinner on.'

'Well, thanks for calling in.'

'No problem. See you soon, Sarah.' She closes the door behind her.

Tonight we'll have to leave, move on once again. Less than twenty-four hours in a place is a new record, even for us.

I open the cupboard under the stairs and looking up at me is Teddy, tears having cleaned two lines down his grubby face. 'I'm sorry, Mama. I couldn't stop it.'

'Don't worry, darling, let's get you cleaned up.'

The Unmothers

I've learned it's best to focus on the details: one woman wears a daffodil-shaped brooch on her lapel; another has a scarf wrapped around her neck in the same purple as my bed sheets; another wears smoky eyeliner, a look I've never been able to pull off. I focus on the pain in my feet, each step pushing the pieces of grit further into my soles. I don't think about the other pain, or the rotten egg weaving down my neck, into my collar. And I definitely don't look at the placards.

My earliest memory is being at a parade. The women on the pavement were smiling and laughing, babies in their bellies, or children by their sides. I stood at the front, my hand in my mother's, watching the other women shuffling down the road. It was my first year at school and I wanted to show Mother how good my reading was. I tugged on her coat, pointed at a big piece of paper placard directly opposite us and tried to sound out the word. 'B-a-r-r-e-n, barren,' I said.

'Don't ever say that word ever again,' she hissed.

'Did I say it wrong?'

'No, but that's not the point.'

'But–'

'No "buts", Penelope. It's a bad word and you can be cursed if you say it out loud.'

'What does it mean?'

She stroked her rounded stomach, leaving my question unanswered.

Now I'm a married woman, I'm no longer a spectator. After my first parade, when I got back home, my new husband put me in the bath and washed my hair. His whisperings: 'We haven't been trying long' and 'There's still plenty of time' were as soothing as the cocoon of warm water. After, he rubbed peppermint cream into my feet and tucked me into bed. Nowadays he doesn't even look up from the TV.

I've only got one more parade, one more year, and then my husband can leave, no questions asked, no fault on his part. He'll be free to meet someone else, start again, try again. I will not. I'll be permanently branded with a red rose, a symbol that life doesn't grow inside me as I continue to bleed monthly.

Hello, Again

The first time I saw her she was lying on the bed, her arms and legs stretched out like a starfish. Having seen every hour the previous night (and several nights before that) I didn't really care that there was a stranger in the house, as long as she didn't want feeding, washing or changing. I lay down on the sliver of bed available and immediately fell asleep. When I woke up, she was gone, and for days I thought she must have been a figment of my imagination. The next time she appeared, Matilda was screaming because she was overdue a feed, but needed changing first. I popped open her babysuit and found that the poo was all the way up her back. 'Great,' I muttered. I opened the drawer of the change table and found no clean nappies.

'Shit!'

'Literally,' a gravelly voice said.

Once upon a time I might have laughed, but I teetered on the fence of emotions and cried instead.

'There, there, no need for tears,' she said, taking a step towards me. 'You know you've got a new pack downstairs.'

'Can you get them for me?'

'No, I can't do that or watch the baby, before you ask.'

'One step ahead of you there.'

I picked up Matilda and stomped down the stairs, trailing drops of poo like Hansel and Gretel's crumbs. I grabbed the bag of nappies and stomped back upstairs, slamming the door shut in her face.

'You're doing that wrong,' she said.

'How did you…?'

She shrugged. 'Magic. You really are doing that wrong though. If you open up the suit wider at the neckline, you can pull it down and then you won't have to get poo in her hair.'

I didn't want her to be right, but she was.

After that, she started appearing more and more often, until she was with us almost every day. I hadn't realised how lonely I was.

One day she told me that she was leaving. Matilda was nearly six months old and the darkness of winter was giving way to spring light.

'Where are you going?'

'I don't know yet.'

'But I need you.'

She took my hand and squeezed it. 'No, you don't. Think back to how things were when I first met you and how you've changed.'

I squeezed her hand, hoping that this simple gesture would convey how grateful I was for everything she'd taught me, how she'd helped me learn to enjoy being a mother. 'I'll miss you,' I said, instead of admitting that she was right.

Let Love Lead the Way

When Jess and I were at school, she was the loud one and I was the quiet one. There were also two more girls in our group: Kelly and Vanessa. They were the tall one and the chubby one. We were like a dumbed-down version of The Spice Girls. We couldn't sing, but rumour had it that neither could they.

Kelly and Vanessa left. I thought our friendship was for life, but it turns out that a couple of hundred miles and a tertiary education is quite a divider. But I still had Jess.

By chance we were pregnant around the same time and thought – foolishly – that that was the hardest thing we'd ever have to do. We compared cravings and discomforts and lack of sleep, all the while looking forward to the birth of our little bundles of joy. Oh, how innocent we were.

The first few months we continued to bemoan our lack of sleep, discomforts and the state of our bodies. We celebrated both babies' accomplishments and told each other what a good job we were doing. The problems started when they got to six, seven months old: the time for weaning and moving around. Jess wouldn't give Archie anything but breast milk, even though the health visitor said to introduce water. 'Oh no, Mummy's milkshake is much better, isn't it, poppet?' she cooed and Archie cooed back. It meant I had to keep moving Daisy's water out of reach.

Archie stole Daisy's toys. He hit, bit, pinched and slapped. Jess never said a word.

'Children need to find their own way.'

'They need boundaries, Jess, they're children,' I said. 'They don't know anything about anything yet.'

'We'll just have to agree to disagree on that one.'

You don't say.

Playdates became impossible. I suggested meeting without the kids, going for a meal or to the cinema like we used to, but she wouldn't leave him. In the end I stopped asking.

Today, we meet again, by the school gate, the same ones we ran through every morning together when we were four years old. I wonder if this is the first time she's leaving him. I smile, shyly, like it's my first day and I'm trying to make a new friend.

She smiles too. 'Alright?'

'Uh huh.'

'Worried about Daisy starting school?'

I nod. 'A little. You?'

'Yeah. Actually,' she says, and takes a step closer. 'Don't tell anyone, but I can't wait.'

I look at her face but there's no indication that this is a trap. 'Me neither.'

We both burst out laughing.

Not all Linings Are Silver

I was going to save up for a First Five Pack (feed, smile, giggle, step, word), but I wasn't sure how long I'd had the baby with me, so I chose a Random Five pack instead.

The first time I see myself cradling a baby, a little girl I named Annabelle, I can't quite believe it's me. I'm probably about fifteen or sixteen. My hair's sweaty, my skin too, and I've got purple smudges under my eyes, but I also look kind of happy, and I wonder whether I wanted to have that baby, and why she's not with me anymore.

The other four are also of just me and her. In one I'm feeding her, her mouth wrapped around my nipple. As soon as I saw this, I whipped my top and bra off, grabbed my boobs and looked for signs that they'd fed a baby. They were slightly droopier than ten years ago, but that's not exactly evidence, not like stretch marks would have been, and there weren't any of those. There aren't any on my tummy either.

In memory three she's sleeping and I'm drifting in and out of sleep myself, but each time I open my eyes she's in a cot by my bed. In the next I'm bathing her. The stump of her umbilical cord is still attached and I'm wiping around it gently with a cotton wool pad. I get them out a lot at first, the memories, but soon I've seen them so many times, I only need to close my eyes to be reminded, which has pros and cons.

It was by chance that I found out I'd had a baby. About six months ago I was in a car accident, and unconscious when I was brought in. Not for long, but by then the bureaucratic cogs had already been set in motion. They did the scan. Lucky some might say, but I say: the jury's still out on that one. Anyway, I still remained pretty out of it for some time, drifting in and out of sleep.

I was just waking up on day three when I heard the doctors talking.

'Results of the scan are back,' a young male voice says. 'Jane Doe's name is Gemma Bridge. She's twenty-six years old, blood type B negative, she's had one leg fracture and no major ops.'

I hear the rustling of some paper. 'You see this, Hunter?' a female voice says. 'This means she's had a baby.'

Baby?

'And this means her memories of it have been wiped,' the female doctor says.

'What the...?' he whispers.

Fuck. That's the word you're looking for.

'There's a blip in her memory timeline where the government have erased her memories of conception, pregnancy, birth and for however long she had the baby.'

The silence is only disturbed by the increasing beep of the monitors.

'So she doesn't know?'

'No, and we're not allowed to tell her either. As doctors, we've signed an oath. You will have covered this in your training.'

'Yes, but I'm not sure I feel comfortable.'

'What you need to remember, Hunter, is that the government say it's for their own good. Most of these children were conceived under violent circumstances or the mothers were deemed too young or unfit to care for them.' Fingers press on my wrist and I assume that the doctor is taking my pulse. 'Often the mothers are orphans or have little in the way of a support network. Gemma was fifteen when she had her baby. She was definitely young. She may also have been unfit.'

'So it's for her own good?' I hear the relief in the lighter tone of his voice.

'That's the idea, and the baby's. The government will no doubt have placed the baby in a good home.'

The fingers creep further around my wrist and squeeze.

'Do you think she'll wake up soon?' he asks.

I squeeze back.

'Oh yes, very soon,' the female doctor says. 'Come on, let's get these rounds done before the canteen runs out of coffee.'

'Does that really happen?'

'No, Hunter,' she sighs. 'The doctors would go on strike.'

The curtains are pulled back round my cubicle and the doctors leave. I'm alone again.

I've heard rumours that these black market memories are fakes, that they only have a limited number to go around and they cut and paste them, selling them on to desperate women who have no recollection of their babies. It might be true, but I can't allow myself to believe that.

The last memory I have of her is that I'm getting her dressed into a pink and white striped baby grow, a pink cardigan and a white woolly hat. I wrap her in a large knitted blanket. We're still at the hospital and she's only a few days old. She just looks at me the whole time, with those muddy-blue eyes of hers, as if she's committing all my features to memory.

As I am hers.

Guilt Trip

'Come in!' a voice shouts from behind a closed door.

Belinda gets up. The discarded flakes of her nail polish fall, scattering like fairy dust, from her lap onto the carpet. She slips into her boss's office.

'Sit,' her boss says, not looking up from her computer.

Belinda perches on the edge of the chair, her wings humming a delicate tune. She looks around at the various awards on the wall. There's one of hers, from when she first graduated and still worked in production. That year she produced more than any other fairy. She's come a long way since.

'You've been busy,' her boss says, large wings opening and closing slowly. 'I knew you were the right person for the job when I promoted you to Head of Distribution last year, but you've exceeded my expectations.'

Belinda's wings beat faster, the tune louder. 'Thank you, Mother Fairy.'

'Keep up the good work. However, the amount of money you're spending on Guilt Dust is through the roof, as I told you at your last review. I'm afraid I'm going to have to issue you with a formal warning.' She pushes a piece of paper across the desk and places a pen on top of it. 'Please sign here to say we've had this discussion.'

Belinda leans forward, but doesn't pick up the pen.

'What are you waiting for?'

'I… I can't achieve my targets on less Guilt Dust, Mother Fairy. I'm only just managing as it is.'

'Costs are costs, Belinda. There's nothing I can do about that.'

'But you've said so yourself, Mother Fairy: the only way to keep the mothers in line is to keep them feeling guilty. If you allow them to feel happy, who knows what could happen.'

'Indeed.' She rests her elbows on the desk. 'Tell me: how are you dealing with the sleepless nights?'

'I lie in wait. They all fall asleep eventually.'

'Not theirs, Belinda. Yours.'

'Oh… uh… training, I suppose.' Her left eyelid flickers and she feels betrayed by her own body.

'Because I don't want you to burn out. You're no use to me if you can't work.'

'No, Mother Fairy.'

She picks up the pen and aims it at Belinda. 'Sign this before you go.'

Belinda closes the door behind her and instead of seeing Mother Fairy's full name and job title in the plaque on her door, all she can see is her own reflection. She rubs her left eye, but the eyelid won't be still. An image of a mother pops up from last night: rocking on a chair, feet curled up trying to keep warm, a screaming baby on her shoulder. After a couple of hours, they had both cried themselves to sleep and Belinda took her chance. Job done.

No-one warned her that she would be haunted by the daytime shadows of the mothers. That she would see them in mirrors, shop windows, puddles, every time she closed her eyes. She reminds herself of how hard she worked to get the job, tells herself that she's doing the right thing. But, on occasion, she lets herself ponder why the previous two fairies left so abruptly and haven't been seen since.

A Bedtime Story

Kim likes to line up her collection of soft toys on her bed along the wall. She says good night to all of them and gives each one a kiss. Then she climbs carefully into bed so as not to disturb any of them. If one of them is knocked over, it can result in tears.

'Story, Mummy.' Kim climbs into bed.

I tuck her in up to her chin and she holds onto the quilt with both hands.

'Which one would you like?' I ask her. She has her favourites, of course, in amongst the vast selection of colourful picture books, but she also enjoys the stories I tell her. Some of them are fictional and others true.

'Can I have the one about the shoes?'

I smile and reach for the pair of baby shoes sitting on her chest of drawers. They are bright red with pink flowers up the sides. I turn them over. The soft soles are for babies who are too young to walk and these ones are clean and white.

'Once upon a time there was a mummy and daddy who loved each other very much and they were very happy. They decided they wanted to share their happiness with a baby and started looking for a very special baby.'

'Where did they look?' Kim grins, knowing how the story goes.

I got down on my hands and knees and looked under the bed. 'Kim,' I say, 'were you under the bed?'

'No!' she shouts.

I walk over to the wardrobe and open the doors. 'Kim, were you in the wardrobe?'

'No,' she shouts again.

I open her bedroom door, put my hand above my eyes and look down the corridor. 'Kim, were you out there?'

She nods. 'Yes, Mummy, I was far, far away.'

'Yes, darling,' I say sit down on the edge of her bed. 'You were a long way away. Daddy and Mummy had to travel by car, by plane and by boat to find you. You were so far away.'

'I was hiding.'

'You were hiding, but we found you, in a little village in Vietnam. And when we finally found you–'

'I was a very special baby!'

I stroke her face. 'You were a very special baby. And I picked you up and said to Daddy: "Here she is. Here's our baby." And we brought you home.'

She yawned, big and unguarded. 'But the shoes, Mummy?'

'Because it had taken us such a long time to find you, the shoes were already too small, but we kept them because they were still your first pair of shoes.'

I reach behind me and put them back on the chest of drawers. I lean over and kiss her forehead. 'Goodnight, darling.'

'Goodnight, Mummy.'

The Motherhood Contract

You must not tell the mother-to-be that she may not instantly love her child.

On the second of April 1997, Elspeth is standing in her dimly lit kitchen doing the washing up. *Don't Speak* by No Doubt comes on the radio and as she leans over to turn the volume up, her waters break, followed by a short burst of pain. She can no longer remember exactly what the midwife said about how many minutes apart or centimetres dilated, so she rings Dave on his newly-acquired-especially-for-this-purpose mobile phone. It goes straight to voicemail. She reverts to the conventional method of ringing the main number and sure enough somebody tracks him down. Within thirty minutes they are on their way to the hospital.

They needn't have hurried. It takes another two days and an emergency caesarean before a screaming baby is born.

Elspeth steals glances at her, and feels nothing.

You must not tell the mother-to-be that breastfeeding hurts.

Breastfeeding is the most natural process in the world, or that's what you're led to believe. Books have been written about it, magazines have printed photos depicting it, and doctors talk about it. But it's a myth.

Elspeth buzzes for a midwife and a blur of blue appears in the room, whipping the baby out of the small cot next to the bed. She flips the baby over one shoulder, holding her in place with one hand. With the other she opens Elspeth's nightgown, and squeezes a breast until thick creamy liquid appears.

'That's your colostrum. Right,' she says, and lays the baby down, wedging some cushions underneath. 'You've got to get the latch right, or nothing'll work properly.'

The baby clamps down.

Elspeth sucks in her breath. 'Should it… hurt this much?'

'Some women find it painful in the beginning.' And the blur of blue disappears.

Days later, Elspeth cries when the baby cries, tears falling gently but steadily down her pale face, knowing what's going to happen. One of the midwives suggests formula, but that isn't an option, because then Elspeth would be a bad mother, failing at the first hurdle.

You must not tell the mother-to-be that the lack of sleep will almost kill her.

The first couple of nights the baby sleeps in chunks of three to four hours and Elspeth feels that at least one part of this process is under control. 'I can do this,' she keeps telling herself.

But then they take the baby home.

'Elspeth,' Dave says, standing over her side of the bed with the baby in his arms. 'Elspeth, I think she needs feeding again.'

'She can't possibly need feeding again.' She looks at the digital numbers glaring out from the bedside cabinet. 'I fed her only two hours ago.'

'I've been walking up and down with her for an hour and she won't go back to sleep. She must be hungry.'

Elspeth rearranges herself in bed and reaches out for the baby. The baby who no longer sleeps in chunks, but merely in slivers, and usually when Elspeth has visitors and then she has to endure comments such as 'Oh, isn't she a good baby?' and in those moments, Elspeth wants to match the baby's screams.

You must not tell the mother-to-be that she will lose herself.

Elspeth feels cheated. No-one warned her that she would no longer recognise herself: physically, mentally, and in every other way. She looks in the mirror and wonders who that person is with pale skin and massive purple globs under her eyes; lank and greasy hair; and a body that still looks six months pregnant months after birth.

Meeting her old friends no longer holds appeal as she has nothing to talk about but the baby, and their frustrations seem so trivial. Meeting the women from her antenatal class is unappealing because all they talk about is babies. And going out without the baby isn't an option.

You must not tell the mother-to-be that her relationship will break down.

When the baby is born, Elspeth and Dave have been together for 291 days. Their relationship which once felt like a luxury cruise ship, large and with a full programme of onboard entertainment, is empty and rusting under the constant battering of a newborn's demands.

Elspeth wants Robert. Having a baby with Robert would have been easy. She would have had the support of their parents. She would have had the comradery of her real friends who would have been having babies around the same time, instead of these forced friendships she has with women who think she's a silly girl for having a baby at twenty-two.

If there was an exam that you needed to pass to be allowed to have a baby – and there should be since it's the only important thing that you do that you don't need to sit an exam for – Elspeth feels that she and Dave would have failed it.

You must not tell the mother-to-be that there will be days when she regrets her decision.

Elspeth wants to turn the clock back, not just to before the baby was born, but to before she was conceived, to that sunny day when she was feeling reckless and aching for something exciting in her life, to when she walked into a pub and out of it with a man who bought her a packet of salt and vinegar crisps.

She wants that comfortable life she was once so scared of; the one in which she knew the rules.

Acknowledgements

Grateful acknowledgment is made to the editors of the following publications in which these works, or earlier versions, previously appeared: 'All the Children', Lunate, 'Breaking the Seal' and 'Near and Far', Spelk, 'That Apple', Fictive Dream, 'The Motherhood Contract', Ellipsis.

The Almost Mothers would not be where it is without the help of those who read (parts of) it in its various stages: Sarah Davy, Gordon Duncan, Anjali Mittal, Damnhait Monaghan, Anne O'Leary and Rebecca Williams, as well as Morgen Bailey whose editing gave it a significant head start. Thank you.

Many thanks to Farhana Shaikh for putting her faith in me and my collection, being an insightful editor and generous mentor.

Huge thanks to all my family and friends, including those in the (online) writing community, for the cheerleading; to my mother-in-law for her support; to my sister for the advice, writing or otherwise; to my mum for reading to me and gifting me my first passion in life; to my husband for being endlessly supportive of my writing, despite the lack of flying monkeys; and to my boys, for being generally awesome and sleeping (sometimes).